W9-CAU-564

TROUE
1890

Cemetery Girl

BOOK ONE: THE PRETENDERS

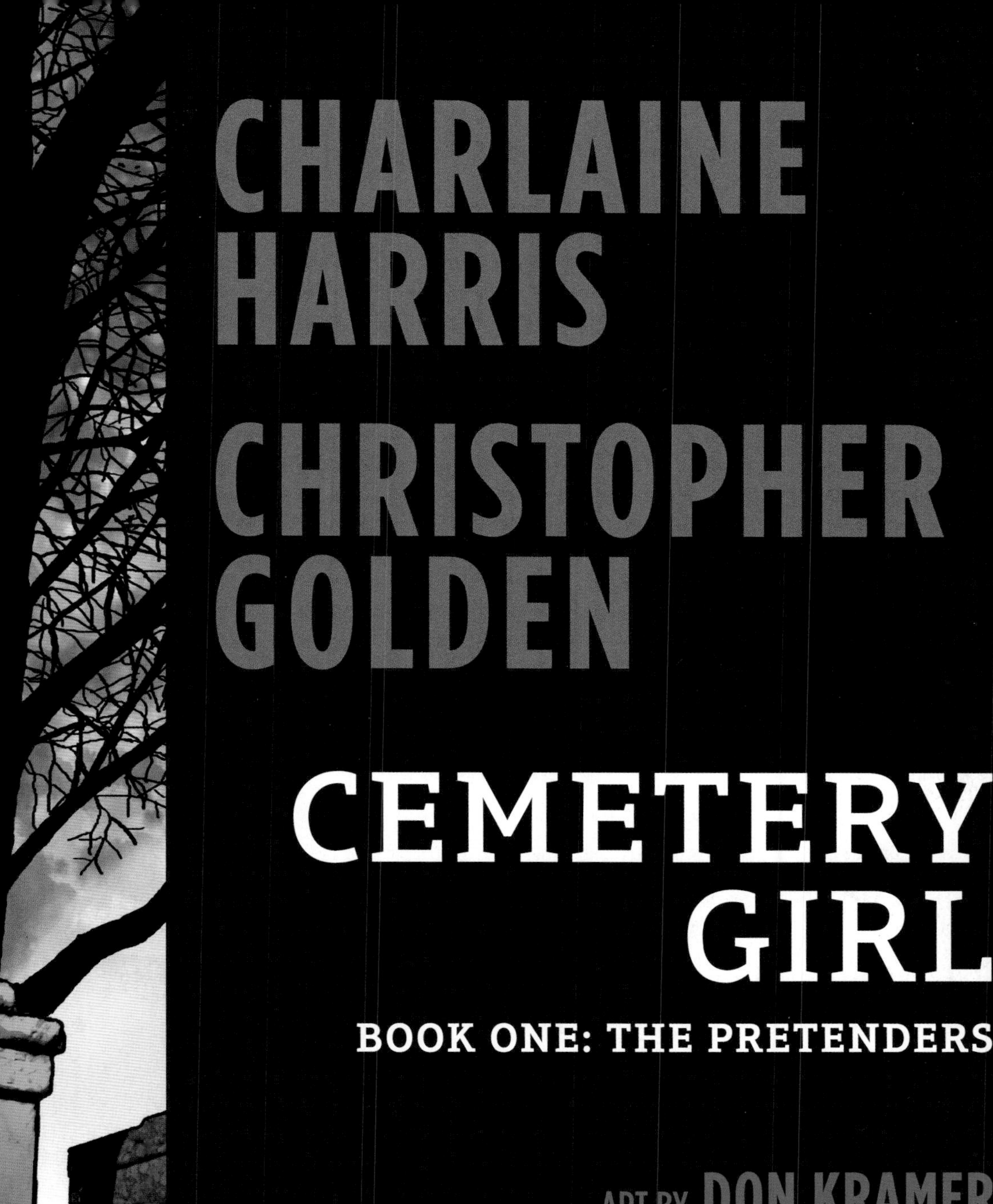

CHARLAINE HARRIS

CHRISTOPHER GOLDEN

CEMETERY GIRL

BOOK ONE: THE PRETENDERS

ART BY **DON KRAMER**

COLORS BY **DANIELE RUDONI**

LETTERS BY **JACOB BASCLE**

THE BERKLEY PUBLISHING GROUP
Published by the Penguin Group
Penguin Group (USA) LLC
375 Hudson Street, New York, New York 10014

USA • Canada • UK • Ireland • Australia • New Zealand • India • South Africa • China

penguin.com

A Penguin Random House Company

This book is an original publication of The Berkley Publishing Group.

Library of Congress Cataloging-in-Publication Data

Harris, Charlaine.
Cemetery girl / Charlaine Harris and Christopher Golden. — First Edition.
pages cm — (The Pretenders ; book 1)
ISBN 978-0-425-25666-4 (hardcover)
1. Cemetery—Fiction. 2. Young women—Fiction. I. Golden, Christopher author. II. Title.
PS3558.A6427C46 2013
813'.54—dc23
2013011424

FIRST EDITION: January 2014

PRINTED IN THE UNITED STATES OF AMERICA

10 9 8 7 6 5 4 3 2 1

Cover illustration by Don Kramer.
Cover design by Jason Gill.
Cover colors by Daniele Rudoni.

NIGHT ONE.
DUNHILL CEMETER
uhnfff

THUNK
SPLISH
I'M PRETTY SURE I DIED.

FOR, LIKE, A MINUTE AT LEAST.
KOFF KOFF
IT'S HARD TO SAY HOW LONG, REALLY.
HARD TO TELL TIME WHEN YOU'RE DEAD, I GUESS.
TORRANCE
COME ON, BRAIN. KICK-START. WHO THE HELL AM I?
KOFF
HOW DID I...?
SKRRRITCHH

THUMPP
OH.
CALEXA
HOLD STILL, BITCH.
THWAK
CALEXA
CAN ONLY REMEMBER FRAGMENTS, BUT I KNOW THIS...
I REALLY AM SUPPOSED TO BE DEAD.

VRRRRMMM
VVRRRMMM
WHOEVER LEFT ME FOR DEAD...
...I DON'T THINK IT WAS THIS GUY. SOME KIND OF CARETAKER OR SOMETHING.
SLAM

NEED SOMEWHERE TO THINK.
SOMEWHERE OUT OF THE RAIN.
SOMEWHERE TO HIDE.
YEAHHH! WOOOO!
GUN IT, DANNY!
I SURE CAN'T GO OUT THERE.

SOMEONE LEFT ME FOR DEAD.
UNTIL I CAN FIGURE OUT WHO THAT WAS...
...AND WHY...
CLANNGG
HOOOO
...I'M GONNA HAVE TO PLAY DEAD.

WHIRRRRR

WHERE...?

CEMETERY. RIGHT.
GREAT.
WHIRRRRR

...I'M SAYIN' I DIDN'T TRAMPLE THE DAMN FLOWERS.
I AIN'T EVEN BEEN OVER THAT SIDE OF THE PLACE THIS MORNIN'.
IT'S THE DAMN KIDS, MAN.

I HAVE TO LEAVE. IF HE NOTICES THE GATE'S BEEN FORCED, HE'LL FIND ME.

WHIRRRRR

AREN'T YOU HOT IN THAT JACKET?
I'M OKAY. NICOTINE KEEPS ME COOL.
RIGHT. KEEP SMOKING THOSE *THINGS,* I'LL BE DRIVING *YOUR* FAMILY TO *YOUR* FUNERAL.
ALL THESE PEOPLE HERE FOR A DEAD PERSON.
ISN'T ANYONE LOOKING FOR ME?

THE FLOOR OF THAT CRYPT IS PRETTY HARD. MAYBE--
CORRONEY
BORN FEBRUARY 28, 1908
DIED OCTOBER 19, 1974
Whoa.

NO WAY.
SO NOW I'M SEEING GHOSTS? SOULS?

I DON'T THINK SEEING THAT STUFF IS NORMAL FOR ANYONE.
UNLESS...MAYBE IT'S NORMAL FOR ME. MAYBE I COULD ALWAYS DO THAT.
HOW WOULD I EVEN KNOW?
IF I CAN'T REMEMBER WHO I AM OR WHERE I COME FROM...MAYBE I'M WORSE OFF THAN THE DEAD GUY.
HE'S GOT A HEADSTONE WITH HIS NAME ON IT. AN IDENTITY. A LIFE...EVEN AFTER DEATH.
HE'LL BE REMEMBERED.

SOMEBODY TRIED TO MURDER ME.
THAT'S SAD AND SCARY. I JUST KNOW WHOEVER DID THIS IS SOMEONE CLOSE TO ME.
A FRIEND. FAMILY, MAYBE. I CAN FEEL IT.
I SHOULD GO TO THE POLICE, BUT THEY WOULD BRING ME HOME. I CAN'T RISK THAT.
IF WHOEVER LEFT ME HERE FINDS OUT I'M ALIVE, MY GUESS IS THAT THEY'LL WANT TO FINISH THE JOB.
SPAULDING SLOVIN
HE LIVED BRIEFLY FOR HIS MUSIC
DEVOTED SON AND BROTHER
BORN
JUNE 21,1969
DIED
JANUARY 12,1991
COLTERE
UNTIL I GET MY MEMORY BACK, THIS MAY BE THE ONLY SAFE PLACE IN THE WORLD FOR ME. HERE WITH THE DEAD.
SO WHAT THE HELL AM I SUPPOSED TO DO IN THE MEANTIME?

NIGHT TWO.
IT WAS PRETTY GREAT, WASN'T IT?
YES, IT WAS, MR. BOOKMAN.
ONE FOR THE ANGELS.

KLIKK
HOVE NISSAN
GMC
ANTHONY KELNER
SORRY, MR. KELNER. I DON'T KNOW MUCH, BUT I KNOW THIS...
...I'M NOT GONNA LAST LONG WITHOUT SOMETHING TO EAT.

RAAWWK! LOVE THE BIRD!
POLICE SEARCH FOR MISSING GIRL CALLED OFF
SLAM

WHA...?
RAAWWK!
TONY. LOVE THE BIRD, TONY.
SHUT UP, STUPID BIRD.
IF JANICE HADN'T LOVED YOU SO MUCH, I'D WRING YOUR NECK.
NOW WHAT THE HELL WAS...?
YOU GOTTA BE KIDDIN' ME.

SERIOUSLY?
THIS IS MY LIFE?
AND YET SOMEHOW I'M MORE AFRAID TO LEAVE THAN I AM TO STAY.
WHICH MEANS UNTIL I FIND OUT WHY SOMEONE WANTS TO KILL ME, I KEEP MY HEAD DOWN. STAY HIDDEN.

BUT THERE ARE OTHER THINGS I'M GOING TO NEED TO SURVIVE.

HONEY, I LEFT THE CAKE IN THE CAR! CAN YOU GET IT?
DID YOU HEAR ME?
I GOT IT. SEE IF YOU CAN FIND BIRTHDAY CANDLES, WILL YOU?
I DON'T LIKE HAVING TO STEAL. DON'T LIKE HOW IT FEELS, DOWN INSIDE ME.
MEREDITH
ALEX
SHOUP
BUT I PREFER IT TO BEING DEAD.

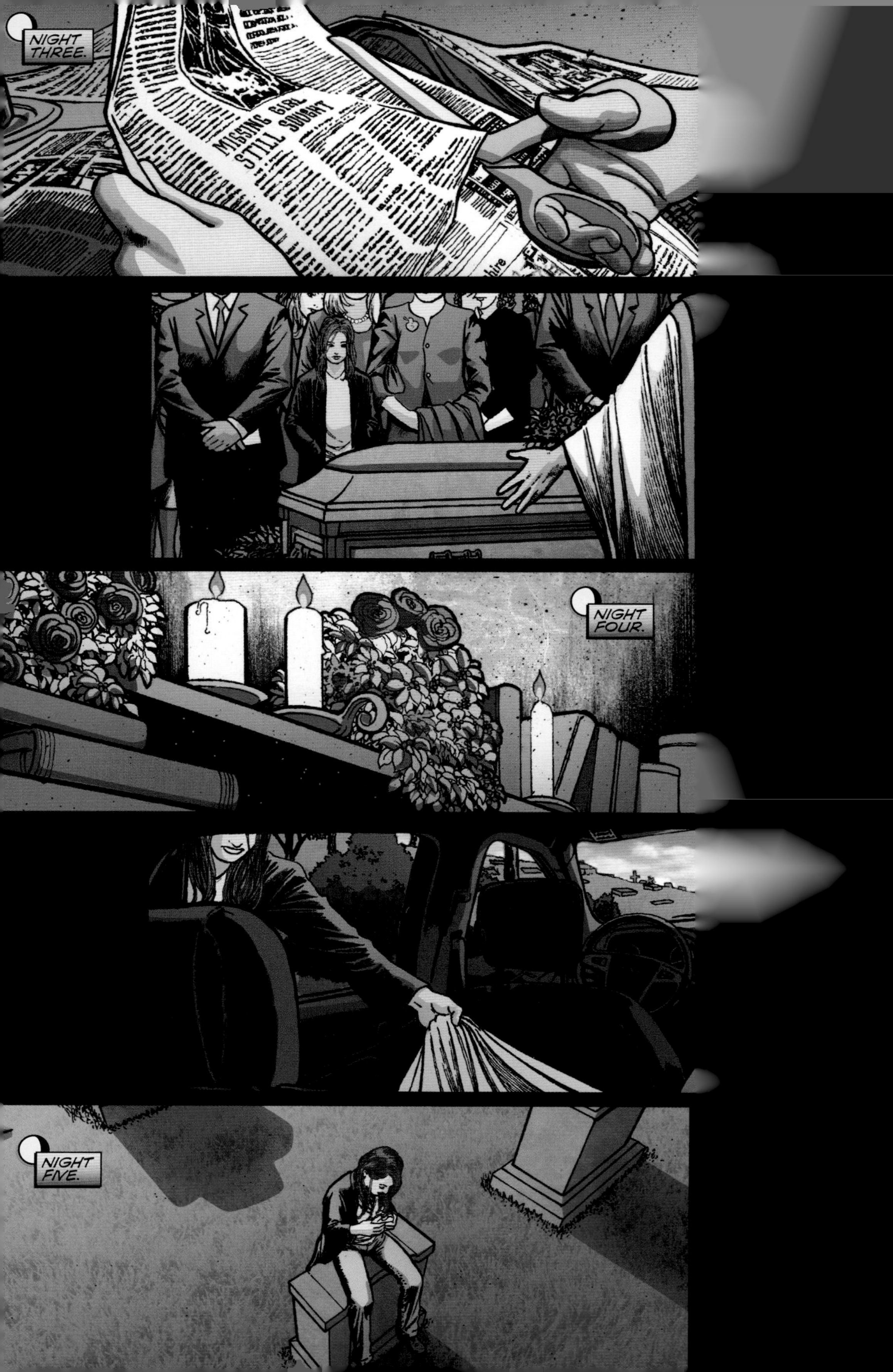
NIGHT THREE.
MISSING GIRL STILL SOUGHT
NIGHT FOUR.
NIGHT FIVE.

CLANNGG
Hunh.
DON'T EVEN BREATHE, OLD MAN.
KID, THIS ISN'T WORTH JAIL TIME. I GOT NOTHING.
WATCH AND WALLET, OLD MAN, AND CELL PHONE IF YOU GOT ONE. OR I'LL PUT YOU IN ONE OF THESE GRAVES.

AAAAAHHH!
CLUNK
WOW.
THANKS, KID. GOOD SAVE.
WHERE'D YOU COME FROM?
I...I DON'T...
IF YOU WERE IN HERE PARTYING... SCOOT.
I GOT TO CALL THE COPS ABOUT THIS IDIOT.
THAT'S ME? THAT'S MY VOICE? IT'S AWFUL.
TONIGHT YOU GOT A FREE PASS.

ROY
THE OLD MAN ASKED WHERE I'M FROM. I DON'T HAVE AN IDENTITY.
THAT'S ONE MORE THING I'M GOING TO HAVE TO STEAL.
A GIRL HAS TO HAVE A NAME, RIGHT?
WHAT'S YOUR NAME?
ANGELA
ROSE.
THAT'S PRETTY.

CALEXA
HMM.
CALEXA
SO NOW I HAVE A NAME.
GOOD EVENING, MISS. PLEASED TO MEET YOU.
OH, ME?
HERE LIES
LINDA BARSI
OVING MEMORY
OF
EL ADER
SHE REST IN PEACE
IN LOVING MEMORY
OF
JAMES OTT
CALEXA ROSE DUNHILL, AT YOUR SERVICE.

IT'S ALWAYS SADDEST LIKE THIS--JUST ONE LONELY PERSON, COMING TO REMEMBER SOMEONE LOVE WON'T LET THEM FORGET.
I LIKE FLOWERS, BUT I NEVER TAKE THE ONES THE LONELY PEOPLE BRING.
IT WOULDN'T BE RIGHT.
NIGHT SIX.
WHOEVER I WAS BEFORE, I'M PRETTY SURE I WASN'T A THIEF.
I'LL MAKE UP FOR IT SOMEDAY. SOMEHOW, I'LL PAY EVERYONE BACK. BUT TONIGHT I'M HUNGRY. A GIRL'S GOTTA EAT.

NIGHT EIGHT.
POLICE THINK MISSING TEEN MAY BE RUNAWAY
NINE.
AMBER ALERT FOR LOCAL GIRL
OPINION
LOCAL K
ASSISTS T
PLANS FO
CONSTRUCTI
NIGHT ELEVEN.
FORMER SENAT
BOB TOWNO
MISSING GIRL STILL SOUGHT

NIGHT THIRTEEN.
I'VE FOUND STORIES ABOUT TWO DIFFERENT MISSING GIRLS IN THE NEWSPAPERS.
ONE OF THEM IS A FOURTEEN-MONTH-OLD BABY, SNATCHED BY HER DAD. THE OTHER'S A THIRTEEN-YEAR-OLD RUNAWAY.
OBVIOUSLY, NEITHER OF THEM IS ME.
MISSING GIRL STILL SOUGHT
AMBER ALERT FOR LOCAL GIRL
RIVER SEARCH FOR MISSING GIRL ABANDONED
IT'S LIKE, AS FAR AS THE WORLD IS CONCERNED, I NEVER EVEN EXISTED.

NIGHT TWENTY-THREE.
HAHA HAHA HAHA HA HA
SHUT UP, YOU IDIOTS! THE OLD MAN WILL HEAR YOU.
CERISE IS RIGHT, MAN. KEEP IT DOWN OR WE'RE BUSTED.
COURSE I'M RIGHT. WHEN AM I NOT?
GIRL, YOU NEED TO CHILL.
YEAH, HAVE YOU MET ME? ME AND CHILL AREN'T EXACTLY BEST FRIENDS.
LIGHT

WILLIE, TREY... THE WHITE CANDLES HAVE TO FORM A CIRCLE. DO YOU EVEN KNOW WHAT A CIRCLE LOOKS LIKE?
THEN YOU GOTTA PUT THE RED CANDLES AT THE POINTS OF THE PENTAGRAM.
YOU REALLY THINK THIS IS GONNA WORK?
NO IDEA. BUT AIN'T THAT THE THRILL? IF IT DOES...
IN LO... MEMORY
BORN ...RY 8, 1917
...WELL, LET'S JUST SAY NOBODY'S GONNA MESS WITH ANY OF US EVER AGAIN.

WILLIE, JOIN THE CIRCLE.
ISN'T THIS, LIKE, BLASPHEMY OR WHATEVER?
GET IN THE DAMN CIRCLE!
A'IGHT. FREAK.
I CONJURE THEE BY THE FIRE OF ORNUNG AND THE BLOOD OF YITHRA. WE CALL THEE BEFORE US, HERE AMONG THE DEAD, IN THE LIGHT OF THE VISIBLE SHADOW.
ZI KYEH RAMLA SHTAH!

ZI KYEH RAMLA SHTAH!
ZI KYEH RAMLA SHTAH!
ZI KYEH RAMLA SHTAH!
ZI KYEH RAMLA SHTAH!
ZI KYEH RAMLA SHTAH!
DAMN, GIRL. CAN'T BELIEVE YOU WENT THROUGH WITH IT.
DID YOU SPREAD THE SALT AROUND LIKE I SHOWED YOU?
DID YOU ASSHOLES SCREW UP THE DAMN PENTAGRAM?
MAYBE IT WASN'T US WHO SCREWED UP. I MEAN, THAT GIBBERISH AIN'T EXACTLY YOUR MOTHER TONGUE.

SCREW YOU!
WHAT THE HELL, CERISE? I KNOW YOU ACTUALLY BUY INTO THIS CRAP, BUT COULD YOU RELAX FOR JUST A--
RELAX? I JUST CUT MY HAND OPEN. I'M BLEEDIN' LIKE HELL, AND IT'S ALL FOR NOTHIN' IF YOU CAN'T FOLLOW SIMPLE DIRECTIONS!
WE SHOULD JUST GO.
BACK OFF, WILL YOU, CERISE? IT DIDN'T WORK 'CAUSE IT DON'T WORK. WE DIDN'T RAISE A DEMON 'CAUSE DEMONS DON'T EXIST.
IF YOU REALLY BELIEVE THAT, WHY ARE YOU EVEN OUT HERE?

WHO DOESN'T LOVE BLACK MAGIC IN A CEMETERY? THERE'S BEER...AND I FIGURED WITCHCRAFT OR WHAT-EVER MIGHT MEAN YOU GOTTA BE NAKED.
THERE'S A LOT OF NAKED CHICKS IN ALL THOSE MOVIES WITH, LIKE, SATANIC RITUALS AND STUFF.
CENTRAL

YOU'RE SUCH AN ASS.
THAT'S WHY YOU LOVE ME.
WE'RE TRYING THIS AGAIN. SOON AS I FIGURE OUT WHY IT DIDN'T WORK, WE'RE COMING BACK.
ACCORDING TO WILLIE, IT DIDN'T WORK 'CAUSE WE AIN'T NAKED.
DAMN, LINA, DON'T ENCOURAGE HIM. NOBODY'S GETTIN' NAKED.
I DON'T KNOW. I'VE SEEN THE SAME MOVIES WILLIE HAS. THE RECIPES FOR THESE THINGS ALWAYS GOT SEX ***AND*** BLOOD.
SMITH

WOW, LINA. YOU ARE SUCH A SLUT.
AND YOU LOVE IT.
WELL, YEAH.
THEY HAD ME CONVINCED FOR A MINUTE.
SCARED ME SO MUCH I WAS HOLDING MY BREATH.
NOW I CAN EXHALE.
JOSHUA MICHAELS
LOVED BY ALL
BORN JANUARY 22, 1964
DIED DECEMBER 14, 1994
ANGELA DAVISON
FOREVER LOVED
AUGUST 30, 1946
JUNE 14, 1974
BUT I'VE GOT TO WATCH THESE KIDS. IF THEY CAUSE ENOUGH TROUBLE IN THE CEMETERY, IT WON'T MATTER HOW CLEVER I AM. THEY'LL GET ME CAUGHT.

SCHRIPPT
PTTHHH
APPARENTLY, I'M NOT BIG ON PARTYING.
UCKK.
GOOD TO KNOW.

NIGHT TWENTY-SIX.

LOCAL MAN ACQUITTE
KLIKK

WHAT IN THE NAME OF...?
THUNK
DON'T MAKE ME BOP YOU ONE.
WAIT, GIRL! YOU GAVE ME A FRIGHT, BUT--
WAIT! WHO ARE YOU?

"WHO ARE YOU?"
STARK
IDONTKNOWI DONTKNOWIDONT KNOWIDONTKNOW IDONTKNOW...
STARK
...IDONT KNOWIDONT KNOWIDONTKNOW IDONTKNOWI DONTKNOW...
STARK
...IDONTKNOW IDONTKNOWIDONT KNOWIDONTKNOWI DONTKNOW...

THIRTY-SEVEN DAYS LATER.

NOT BAD.
THIS SHOULD DO FOR WILLIE.

I AM THE RESURRECTION AND THE LIFE.
FROM WHAT I SAW OF HIM THAT NIGHT HE AND HIS FRIENDS CAME TO PLAY "BLACK-MAGIC DRESS-UP," WILLIE WAS KIND OF AN ASSHOLE.
BUT THE DRUNK WHO RAN HIM DOWN IS AN EVEN BIGGER ASSHOLE.
I KNOW WE'LL ALL END UP HERE SOONER OR LATER. IT'S JUST THE "SOONER" I'M TRYING TO AVOID.
LIKE ALL THE OTHERS I'VE WATCHED, WILLIE'S SOUL GOES SOMEPLACE WHEN THE RITUAL BLESSING IS PERFORMED, A BIRD ESCAPING ITS CAGE.
I DON'T KNOW WHERE THEY GO. THE SPIRITS, I MEAN...
BUT IT'S CLEAR THERE'S **SOMETHING** AFTER DEATH.

NIGHT SIXTY-THREE.
IT'S ONLY BEEN A COUPLE OF MONTHS, BUT I'VE BUILT MYSELF A KIND OF LIFE HERE. THE OLD MAN AND I SHARE THIS CEMETERY.
AND WE GUARD IT.
SOMETIMES I'M CONVINCED HE KNOWS I'M HERE.
ZZZZZ...
THAT HE INDULGES ME.
OTHER DAYS, I THINK HE WORKS TOO HARD AND SLEEPS TOO MUCH TO NOTICE.
MY GHOSTLY FRIEND WAS HERE AGAIN. WHAT DO YOU THINK, STUPID BIRD?
SHOULD I REPORT HER? DON'T KNOW IF I COULD LIVE WITH HER ENDING UP IN SOME FOSTER HOME.

NIGHT SIXTY-FIVE.
IT'S A STRANGE SORT OF LIFE.
BUT IT'S SAFE HERE, WITH THE DEAD.
KLIKK
KEEP AN EYE OUT. WE GET SPOTTED GOING IN, AND THIS IS OVER BEFORE IT STARTS.

WHAT THE HELL'S THIS, NOW?
GLAD YOU CAME WITH US, MARLA. WE NEED YOU TONIGHT.
YOU REALLY THINK YOU CAN TALK TO WILLIE? YOU'RE NOT BULLSHITTIN' ME?

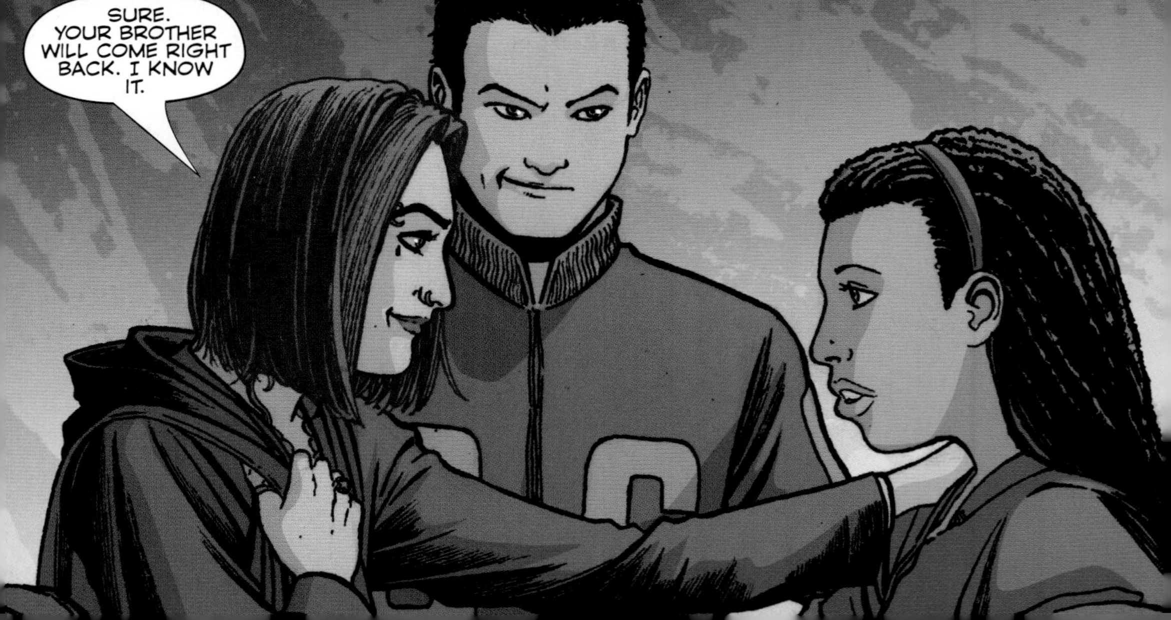
SURE. YOUR BROTHER WILL COME RIGHT BACK. I KNOW IT.

WHAT ARE THEY UP TO? NOT DRINKING, NOT THIS TIME...
I BEEN DOING SOME STUDYING WITH THE BRUJO ON MACKLIN STREET.
HEY, LITTLE GIRL, PUT THE PHONE AWAY.
WE GOT TO GET DOWN TO BUSINESS.
FINE. SO, WHAT NOW?
WILLIAM JESUS VASQUEZ
LOVING SON AND BROTHER
REST IN PEACE
YOU WANT TO SEE YOUR BROTHER AGAIN, YOU GOT TO DO EXACTLY WHAT I SAY.
WHAT'S THE KNIFE FOR?
GOOD QUESTION.

MARLA, YOU GOTTA KNOW WE'RE DOING THIS FOR WILLIE.
COURSE I KNOW--
WHAT THE HELL?
RELAX, HONEY. THIS IS ALL PART OF THE RITUAL.
GET YOUR HANDS OFF ME, BITCH!
CERISE SAYS WE GOTTA ACT THIS THING OUT LIKE WE BELIEVE IT, IF WE WANT WILLIE BACK.
DON'T YOU THINK I WANT MY BROTHER ALIVE AGAIN?
THEN BE STILL, GIRL.

DORI'S IN JAIL, SO WE CAN'T DO NOTHING BUT WAIT ON HER. BUT WILLIE? WE DON'T HAVE TO WAIT FOR HIM.
THE BRUJO TAUGHT ME A WAY TO BRING HIM BACK.
ACCUSATIUM TUAM, EGO SUMMATIA...
THE BRUJO OBVIOUSLY NEVER TOOK LATIN.

BUT I DID?
IT'S SO WEIRD, THE THINGS I KNOW AND CAN'T

GET 'ER ON THE GROUND.
AND HOLD 'ER THERE.
DON'T TOUCH ME! JUST TELL ME WHAT YOU NEED ME TO DO!

THAT'S AN EASY ONE, MARLS...

WE NEED YOU TO DIE.

NO WAY.
THEY KNOW THAT BLACK-MAGIC STUFF DOESN'T WORK.
THEY'RE PRETENDING... LIKE BEFORE.

NOOOOOOO!
BUT THIS GIRL DOESN'T THINK SO.

I HAVE TO...

EGO... VITUALMEN VOX UT ERIGO... UNUS...VESTRY... CRUOR!
CERISE, NO!
AAAIIIIIIEEEEEEE!
OH MY GOD, CERISE, YOU...
YOU CRAZY BITCH, YOU KILLED HER!
NO, WE KILLED HER. TO GET WILLIE BACK, JUST LIKE I SAID.
YOU SAID WE JUST HAD TO PRETEND, THAT THE RITUAL WAS JUST--
I TOLD YOU WHAT YOU WANTED TO BELIEVE. BUT YOU ALL KNOW BETTER THAN THAT.
YOU'RE TRYING TO RAISE SOMEONE FROM THE DEAD, AND YOU THOUGHT YOU COULD DO IT WITHOUT SPILLING BLOOD?
WITHOUT GIVING A LIFE IN RETURN?
AND HOW'S THAT WORKING OUT, CERISE?

MARLA'S DEAD, AND I DON'T SEE WILLIE CLIMBING OUT OF HIS DAMN GRAVE!
AND WHAT ARE WE SUPPOSED TO DO WITH MARLA NOW?
WHAT DO YOU THINK, ASSHOLE?
BURY HER.
SO MUCH FOR MAGIC. POOR WILLIE.
THE HELL WITH WILLIE. WE JUST KILLED MARLA FOR NOTHING. WE'RE SO--
SHUT UP AND DIG.
OOOOOHHHH...
WHAT THE...?
OOOHH...
THIS ISN'T HOW IT HAPPENS.

ONCE THE BODY'S BURIED IN SACRED GROUND, THE SOUL GOES ON TO...WHEREVER.
THIS ISN'T RIGHT!
OOOOOHHHH...
UHNFFFF!

GIVE IT A TRY, *CHICA*. IT AIN'T GONNA KILL YA.
SWAKK
MAYBE A BEER WON'T KILL HER, BUT YOU TRY 'N' GET MY SISTER WASTED, AND I ***WILL*** KILL YOU.
THIS AIN'T ONE OF YOUR NEIGHBORHOOD GIRLS, TREY.
IT AIN'T LIKE THAT, WILLIE.
DAMN RIGHT. AND IT AIN'T EVER GONNA BE.
I CAN MAKE MY OWN DECISIONS, WILLIE.
I'M NOT A LITTLE KID, Y'KNOW.
YOU'RE MY LITTLE SISTER, MARLS.
NO MATTER HOW OLD YOU ARE.

ALL THIS TIME I'VE BEEN WAITING FOR MY MEMORY TO COME BACK.
NOW I'VE GOT A HEAD FULL OF MEMORIES...AND NONE OF THEM ARE MINE.

EEN VICTIM OF HIT AND RUN
WHAT IF I COULD BRING HIM BACK?

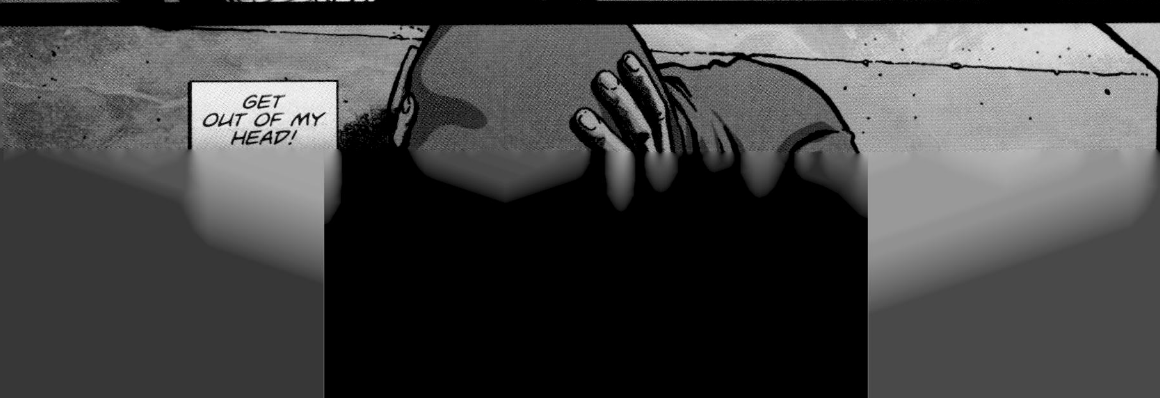
GET OUT OF MY HEAD!

I DON'T UNDERSTAND.
EVER SINCE THE NIGHT I DIED-- JUST FOR A MINUTE--I'VE BEEN ABLE TO SEE THE SPIRITS OF THE DEAD RISE ONCE THEIR BODIES ARE LAID TO REST.
SMITH

I'VE WATCHED DOZENS OF SOULS MOVE FROM THIS WORLD TO WHEREVER IT IS THEY GO NEXT.

BUT THIS GIRL DIDN'T GO ANYWHERE.

SHE'S IN ME.

WHY?
WHAT MAKES YOU DIFFERENT, MARLA? WHAT DO YOU WANT WITH ME?
HOW IS ANY OF THIS EVEN--

BZZZT BZZZT

9:37 PM
Edit
Mom
I'LL B FINE, MOM.
WHEN ARE U COMING HOME?

NIGHT SIXTY-SIX.
MISSING
MISSING:
IT WOULD BE EASIER IF YOU WOULD JUST OPEN UP A LITTLE AND HELP ME TO UNDERSTAND.
I KNOW YOU PREFER TO BE SILENT, CALEXA, BUT I CAN SEE HOW UPSET YOU ARE.
I'M SORRY. IT'S JUST THAT WHENEVER I TALK...I *HATE* THE SOUND.
BUT WHY? IT'S YOUR OWN VOICE.

NO.

It's the voice of a stranger.

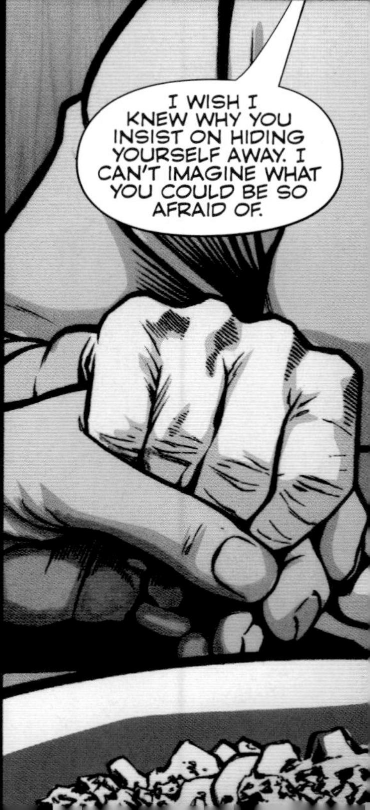
I WISH I KNEW WHY YOU INSIST ON HIDING YOURSELF AWAY. I CAN'T IMAGINE WHAT YOU COULD BE SO AFRAID OF.

LUCINDA...
WHAT... OR WHO.
HER NAME IS LUCINDA CAMERON.
SHE'S SEVENTY-TWO YEARS OLD AND HAS DECIDED TO MAKE ME HER PROJECT.
REMEMBER TO REFOLD YOUR NAPKIN, YOUNG LADY.
ON THAT NIGHT WHEN SHE CAUGHT ME IN HER KITCHEN, SHE FOLLOWED ME OUT AND SAW ME GOING BACK OVER THE WALL.
EXACTLY RIGHT.
NOW, IF YOU DON'T MIND GIVING ME A HAND...
I KEEP CHECKING THE PAPERS. NOTHING YET, BUT I'M SURE I'LL RUN ACROSS SOMETHING ABOUT YOU EVENTUALLY.
SHE COULD HAVE CALLED THE POLICE. INSTEAD, SHE STARTED LEAVING LITTLE BOXES OF FOOD AND SOMETIMES CLOTHES ON HER FRONT STEPS, EACH TAGGED WITH A NOTE.

"FOR THE CEMETERY GIRL."
DON'T YOU WORRY. SOMEDAY YOUR PEOPLE WILL FIND YOU.
BUT WHAT NOW?
I WITNESSED A MURDER.
DOESN'T THAT CHANGE EVERYTHING?
YOU HAD A BIG FAMILY.
ONCE UPON A TIME. FAMILIES AREN'T ALWAYS CLOSE.
OR DON'T ALWAYS STAY CLOSE.
I'M NOT SURE I WANT MY FAMILY TO FIND ME. I DON'T WANT ANYONE TO FIND ME... AT LEAST NOT YET.
I KNOW YOU DON'T WANT TO TALK ABOUT IT, BUT WHEN YOU'RE READY, I'LL BE HERE TO LISTEN. I JUST KNOW SOMEONE IS WONDERING WHERE YOU ARE.
THAT'S WHAT I'M AFRAID OF.

I THOUGHT THE GHOST OF DUNHILL CEMETERY MIGHT NEED A NEW OUTFIT.
THE KILLERS HAVE TO PAY FOR WHAT THEY'VE DONE.
BUT IF I TELL...WHAT HAPPENS TO ME?
I'M AFRAID THE SHOES THAT WENT WITH IT HAVE FALLEN APART. AUNT NETTIE WAS ALWAYS HARD ON HER FEET...
WHAT IS IT, CHILD? WHAT'S WRONG?

ARE YOU ALL RIGHT, DEAR?
I'M... I...
FOR GOODNESS' SAKE, WHAT *IS* IT?

I HAVE TO GET THIS GIRL OUT OF ME. I HAVE TO BE ALONE INSIDE MY SKIN, OR I'LL GO COMPLETELY CRAZY.
NOTHING.
IT'S NOTHING.

I THINK YOU NEED TO LIE DOWN. JUST UNTIL YOU FEEL BETTER.
I SHOULDN'T STAY HERE. I JUST NEED A MINUTE, AND THEN I'LL GO BACK TO THE CEMETERY.
JUST A MINUTE...
ZZZZZZZZZ

WHY ARE YOU JUST STANDING HERE?
Oh my God.
YOU GOTTA DO SOMETHING. YOU KNOW WHAT'S GONNA HAPPEN. WHY DON'T YOU STOP THEM?
NO...I DIDN'T... I DIDN'T KNOW.
I THOUGHT THEY WERE JUST PRETENDING...
...LIKE BEFORE.
I KNOW, CALEXA. AND I DON'T BLAME YOU.
NOT FOR THAT, AND NOT FOR WHAT'S HAPPENING NOW.
THERE'S A HOLLOW PLACE INSIDE YOU, A DEAD SPOT.

IT'S LIKE YOUR SOUL MOVED THE FURNITURE AROUND THE HOUSE AND LEFT AN EMPTY ROOM.
I COULD FEEL THAT EMPTY ROOM CALLING ME, PULLIN' AT ME ALMOST AS MUCH AS WHATEVER-COMES-AFTER WAS PULLIN' AT ME.

I WAS SO SCARED. I DIDN'T WANNA GO, SO I LET THE EMPTY ROOM PULL ME IN.

BUT NOW I'M IN YOU, CALEXA.
I'M TRAPPED HERE, FILLIN' UP THE HOLLOW SPOTS IN YOU, AND I CAN'T GET OUT.

THAT EMPTY ROOM INSIDE YOU IS A HAUNTED HOUSE.

AND I'M THE GHOST.

WHAT ARE YOU GONNA DO, CALEXA?
'CAUSE UNTIL YOU FIND ANOTHER PLACE FOR ME TO GO...
...this ain't over.
uhnff
Oh.
CALEXA, WHAT'S WRONG, HONEY? ARE YOU ILL?
OH.

Marla
47 Missed Calls
93 Text Messages
Close
Clear Alerts

I SHOULD CALL HER MOTHER. CALL SOMEONE.
ZACH

BUT THAT WILL LEAD THE POLICE HERE, AND I'M THE ONLY WITNESS.
I'LL BE GIVING MYSELF AWAY.
WAIT... WHAT'S THIS?
"Hey, little girl, put the phone away. We got to get down to business."
"You want to see your brother again, you got to do exactly what I say."
"What's the knife for?"
HOLY SHIT.

SHE VIDEOED THE WHOLE THING.

Mom
mobile
Decline
BE DOOP DOOP
AAHHH!
MARLA? MARLA? IT'S MOM!
TRUTEL 3G
mobile
End Call
WHAT AM I SUPPOSED TO DO?

I PRAY FOR GUIDANCE.
BUT I'VE BEEN PRAYING FOR ANSWERS FOR THE PAST TWO MONTHS WITHOUT AN ANSWER. TODAY'S NO DIFFERENT.

SO I ASK MARLA'S FORGIVENESS INSTEAD.
OR AT LEAST HER PATIENCE.
"Cerise says we gotta act this thing out like we believe it, if we want Willie back."
GOOD MORNING, YOUNG LADY.
DON'T SUPPOSE YOU WANT TO GIVE ME A HAND?

A.M.HERTZ
PHILLIPS

NO, I DIDN'T FIGURE YOU DID.
NICE TO KNOW MY LITTLE GHOST IS STILL LURKING ABOUT, THOUGH.

Whoops.
Gettin' clumsier every day.

FOR SUCH A CRANKY OLD MAN, KELNER'S REALLY KINDA SWEET.

ALWAYS DROPPING THINGS AT THE MOST OPPORTUNE TIMES. AND I KNOW JUST WHAT TO DO WITH THIS.

IT TOOK ME WEEKS BEFORE I LEFT THE AREA AROUND THE CEMETERY FOR THE FIRST TIME. EVERY TIME, IT'S A RISK I'LL BE RECOGNIZED.
FOOD
KELLY SWARTZ BATTRELL
ANTIQUES
ANGIE DAVIS BAKERY
BUT IF I DON'T GO OUT ONCE IN A WHILE, I'LL GO COMPLETELY NUTS.
SO I MAKE MYSELF AS INVISIBLE AS POSSIBLE, AND I TRY NOT TO BE NOTICED.
BIG ART'S BURGERS
WHO'S NEXT?
BUT BIG ART'S BURGERS ARE A LITTLE PIECE OF HEAVEN.
WELL, WELL.
IT'S BEEN TOO LONG SINCE YOU'VE BEEN IN TO SEE US, HONEY. DON'T BE SUCH A STRANGER.

EVERY TIME I LEAVE THE CEMETERY, I WONDER IF I'M RISKING EVERYTHING ON PURPOSE... IF I WANT TO BE RECOGNIZED...
...TO BE FOUND, EVEN KNOWING IT MIGHT COST MY LIFE. MAYBE IT'S JUST THAT I WANT IT OVER, ONE WAY OR THE OTHER.

AND THEN THIS HAPPENS...
HOW'S IT GOIN'?
HEY, HEY. WAIT. WHAT'D I DO?
DON'T BE LIKE THAT.

I'VE SEEN YOU IN HERE BEFORE, Y'KNOW. I JUST WANTED TO TALK TO YOU.
D'YOU LIVE CLOSE BY?
C'MON, HONEY. HE'S JUST CURIOUS. ME, TOO.
I KNOW THE WHOLE EMO THING'S BEEN DEAD FOR YEARS, BUT THIS GRIM LOOK WORKS FOR YOU.

ESTEBAN, TALK TO HER. MAYBE SHE DON'T SPEAK ENGLISH.

ES VERDAD, CHICA? NO HABLAS INGLÉS?
OR ARE YOU JUST ITCHIN' TO PUT DISTANCE BETWEEN YOURSELF AND THESE SHITHEADS?

I CAN FEEL MARLA'S SHOCK AS SHE RECOGNIZES HIM...I CAN FEEL HER SCREAMING INSIDE ME!

NO! STAY AWAY! GET AWAY FROM HIM!!

AAAAAHHH!
WHAT THE HELL??!!
DAMN, GIRL!

NIGHT SIXTY-SEVEN.
HE'S ONE OF THEM! AT WILLIE'S FUNERAL HE LOOKED RIGHT AT ME! WHAT IF HE RECOGNIZED ME?
STUPID, STUPID GIRL.
THEY DON'T EVEN KNOW YOU SAW THE MURDER, BUT YOU HAVE TO TOTALLY FREAK OUT IN FRONT OF HIM.
NOW HE'LL NEVER FORGET WHAT YOU LOOK LIKE. AND HE'S GOT TO BE WONDERING WHAT MADE YOU LOSE IT LIKE THAT.
WHAT IF HE STARTS TO PUT IT TOGETHER?
WHAT IF HE FIGURES OUT WHERE YOU LIVE?
THEY'RE KILLERS, CALEXA.
ZACH
KILLERS.

YOU GOTTA HELP ME NOW. YOU GOTTA LET ME GO.
I'M NOT HOLDING YOU HERE.
IN A WAY YOU ARE.
THEY KNOW I'M NEVER COMIN' HOME.
THEY AIN'T GONNA ADMIT IT, BUT THEY KNOW.
CAMMY'S PIZZA
DINE IN OR CARRY OUT
THEY KNOW I'D NEVER RUN AWAY, AND NOW IT'S BEEN DAYS. THEY KNOW SOMETHIN' AWFUL HAS HAPPENED.
THE ONLY THING WORSE THAN THE TRUTH IS NEVER KNOWIN' FOR SURE. YOU CAN'T DO THAT TO THEM.
MY PARENTS ALREADY LOST WILLIE. AND MY FRIENDS...
YOU LEAVE ME BURIED IN THAT GRAVE WITHOUT ANY MARKER ON IT, WITHOUT ANYONE KNOWIN' WHAT HAPPENED TO ME...
...THEY'LL NEVER BE ABLE TO LET ME GO.
AND NEITHER WILL YOU.

HOWEVER THIS HAPPENED...
...WE'RE TIED TOGETHER.
NO. PLEASE.
I'M NOT AFRAID OF BEING DEAD ANYMORE, CALEXA. I WANNA SEE WHAT COMES NEXT. I DON'T WANNA BE TRAPPED IN HERE WITH YOU...
...set me free...
ALLEN

OWWWWW
LET'S JUST GET A BANDAGE FOR THAT, HONEY.
NOBODY CRIES OVER A LITTLE CUT LIKE THAT, YOUNG LADY. I HOPE ONE OF THESE DAYS YOU'LL TELL ME WHAT'S ON YOUR MIND.
UNTIL THEN, I JUST HAVE TO GUESS.
SEE HOW WORRIED PEOPL ARE ABOUT THIS GIRL? SOMEONE THAT WORRIED ABO YOU. I JUST KNOW IT.
I JU KNOW

OVER SEVENTY PHONE TIPS. AUTHORITIES ARE ASKING FOR HELP ON TV. TWO HUNDRED VOLUNTEERS SEARCHING!
IT'S NOT LIKE I CAN BE JEALOUS. AFTER ALL, SHE'S DEAD.
AT LEAST, MOSTLY DEAD.

NIGHT SIXTY-EIGHT.
SHE'S GOING TO HAUNT ME UNTIL I DO SOMETHING TO HELP HER. SO SHE CAN BE AT PEACE.
BUT HOW CAN I SHOW PEOPLE WHERE SHE IS WITHOUT GETTING FOUND MYSELF?
NO, AUNTIE. NO LUCK FINDING MARLA TODAY. WORD IS, SOMEONE SAW HER BY THE TRAIN YARD, SO WE WERE SEARCHING OVER THERE.
VOLUNTEER
OH, NO. WHAT THE HELL'S SHE DOING HERE?
THERE'S TALK SHE RAN OFF WITH SOME BOY.

SOUNDS LIKE CERISE IS TRYING TO KEEP THE SEARCH AWAY FROM THE CEMETERY, BUT THAT CAN'T LAST FOREVER. EVENTUALLY, THE BODY WILL BE FOUND.
THEN THE COPS WILL BE EVERYWHERE... THEY'LL FIND ME FOR SURE.
WHAT IF THEY THINK I DID IT?
YOU KNOW WHAT TODAY IS, STUPID BIRD? IT'S THE DAY I MISS HER THE MOST.
♬ Happy ♪ birthday, dear Janice. Happy ♫ birthday to ♫ you.
STUPID BIRD!
SQUAWK!
HAPPY BIRTHDAY!
BOURBON COUNTY
I CAN'T TELL KELNER OR LUCINDA. IF THEY KNOW I'M IN DANGER, THEY'LL DEFINITELY BRING THE POLICE INTO IT, AND I'M JUST NOT READY FOR THAT YET.
BUT FOR THE FIRST TIME, I THINK I CAN ACTUALLY IMAGINE A TIME WHEN I **WILL** BE. MAYBE LUCINDA'S RIGHT...
MAYBE EVERYONE'S GOT SOMEONE WHO'D MISS THEM IF THEY WERE GONE.
EVEN ME.

PHONE'S GOTTA BE AROUND HERE SOMEWHERE.
Keep it down, asshole.

WE HAD TO COME OUT TONIGHT, IN THE DAMN RAIN?
I DON'T KNOW WHY WE'RE LOOKING FOR THE PHONE ANYWAY. IT'S LOST.
WERE YOU NOT *LISTENING* BEFORE?
YEAH, I HEARD YOU. MARLA'S MOMS HAS BEEN CALLIN' HER PHONE, AND SOMEONE PICKED UP. SO *WHAT*?
SO WHAT?
SO WE FIGURED WE BURIED MARLA'S PHONE *WITH* HER, BUT SOMEBODY'S *GOT* THAT PHONE. WE DON'T KNOW WHAT THE BITCH HAD ON IT.

YOU MADE HER PUT IT AWAY, CERISE.
BESIDES, IF SOMEBODY FOUND IT AND TOOK OFF WITH IT, WHAT'RE WE GONNA FIND HERE?
WE KNOW THE LITTLE BITCH TOOK PICS OF US WHEN WE FIRST GOT HERE THAT NIGHT. THAT'S ALL IT'LL TAKE TO PUT US RIGHT IN THE MIDDLE OF THIS SHIT.
YOU DON'T THINK IT WAS KILLIN' HER IN THE FIRST PLACE THAT GOT US INTO THIS?
I WANTED WILLIE BACK. I WOULD'VE DONE ANYTHING--
YEAH, BUT IT DIDN'T WORK, DID IT? WILLIE'S STILL DEAD, AND WE'RE ALL GONNA GO DOWN FOR WHAT YOU DID.
SO DAMN STUPID, FORGETTIN' ABOUT THAT PHONE.
WASN'T TILL HER MOMS MENTIONED SOMEONE PICKING UP THAT I REALLY STARTED THINKING ABOUT IT.

YOU WERE JUST AS FREAKED AS THE REST OF US. YOU PLAY AT BEING THE ICE QUEEN, CERISE, BUT YOU FORGET WE KNOWN YOU ALMOST ALL YOUR LIFE.
ONCE THE KILLING WAS DONE...ONCE WE GOT BLOOD ON OUR HANDS, THAT WAS DIFFERENT THAN JUST TALKIN' ABOUT IT.
WE ALL LOST OUR SHIT FOR A WHILE THERE.
LET'S JUST MAKE SURE WE DON'T BURN FOR IT.
GOTTA SAY, THOUGH... IF SOMEONE PICKED UP THAT PHONE, IT'S LONG GONE.
YOU DON'T KNOW THAT. WE'VE GOTTA AT LEAST LOOK.
WE SEARCH THIS WHOLE AREA. IT AIN'T HERE, WE GOT TO START THINKIN' ABOUT WHO MIGHTA FOUND IT.
THE CARETAKER. MAYBE THE GUYS WHO CUT THE GRASS AND SHIT.
RAIN'S COMIN' DOWN HARDER. THIS AIN'T WORKIN'.
IF IT'S ANYWHERE AROUND HERE, THE BEST WAY TO FIND A CELL PHONE IS TO CALL IT.

LA-LA-LAAA-LA
LA-LA-LAAA-LA
DID YOU HEAR SOME-THING?
No, no! Shut up!
LA-LA-LAAA-LA
LA-LA-LAAA-LA
TRUTEL 3G
9:45 PM
Esteban
mobile
Decline
KLIKK
JOHNSEN
ESTEBAN KNOWS MARLA'S DEAD. SO WHY THE HELL IS HE CALLING HER?

ESS
'RE...
CALL IT AGAIN.
I THINK IT WAS UP THIS WAY.
...HERE!
OVER THERE!
THERE'S SOMEONE ELSE HERE!
N'T KEEP
ALL NIGHT.
USE MARLA'S
ALL THE COPS,
BE ALL OVER
EMETERY.
I'M AFRAID TO TURN IN MARLA'S KILLER BECAUSE I'M AFRAID MY OWN MIGHT FIND ME.

IRONY SUCKS.
BRRRINNG BRRRINNG
H-HELLO?
Marla?

WHAT'D SHE SAY?
SHE... SHE SAID WE GOTTA GET OUT OF HERE.

IDIOT! IT'S NOT MARLA'S GHOST!
JUST SOME BITCH CALLING YOU FROM HER PHONE!

GO FIND HER!

UH-OH.
THAT DEFINITELY DIDN'T WORK OUT LIKE I PLANNED.

EVEN A LIFE IN A CEMETERY...
...IS BETTER THAN NO LIFE AT ALL.
I CAN SMELL YOUUUUU...

GET THE BITCH!!!
THUNKK
AHHHH!
I THINK YOU GOT HER, ESTEBAN. LOOK EVERY-WHERE! SHE'S CLOSE!

GOD, I DON'T WANT TO DIE LIKE THIS.

ALL RIGHT, ASSHOLES! GET OUTTA HERE THE WAY YOU GOT IN, 'CAUSE THE COPS ARE COMING.
I DON'T KNOW YA! LET'S KEEP IT THAT WAY!

OKAY, LITTLE GHOST, I KNOW YOU DON'T WANNA TALK TO ME, BUT I HOPE YOU'RE NOT HURT.

THANKS, KELNER.
YOU'RE A GOOD GUY.
OKAY. HAVE IT YOUR WAY. BUT YOU NEED ANYTHING, YOU COME SEE ME. YOU DON'T NEED TO SAY A WORD.
OH, BY THE WAY, I DIDN'T REALLY CALL THE POLICE.
I SHOULD CALL CHILD SERVICES, Y'KNOW. BUT I GREW UP IN THOSE HOMES, AND I FIGURE YOU'RE BETTER OFF HERE. AT LEAST I CAN KEEP AN EYE ON YOU.
WHEN THE TIME COMES AND YOU'RE READY TO FACE THE WORLD, YOU LET ME KNOW. I'LL HELP THE BEST I CAN. BUT TAKE YOUR TIME, DARLIN'. NO RUSH.
I FIGURE IF YOU GOT TO LIVE IN A CEMETERY, HOME MUST BE PRETTY BAD.
ENOUGH OF THIS.
JUST... ENOUGH.
ZACH

CASPARY

OHHH.
IT'S TIME.

OHMYGOD.
SOME OF THOSE MEMORIES... THEY WEREN'T MARLA'S.

I STAYED UP HALF THE NIGHT, HOPING MORE OF MY MEMORIES WOULD COME BACK. I FIGURE SOMETHING ABOUT HAVING MARLA IN HERE WITH ME MUST'VE SHAKEN THEM LOOSE.

I WANT THEM BACK.
I WANT TO KNOW WHO I REALLY AM--WHO I USED TO BE.
BUT AT THE SAME TIME I'M AFRAID OF WHAT I'LL LEARN.

NONE OF THAT MATTERS TODAY. MY MEMORIES WILL COME BACK OR THEY WON'T.
SCHULTZ

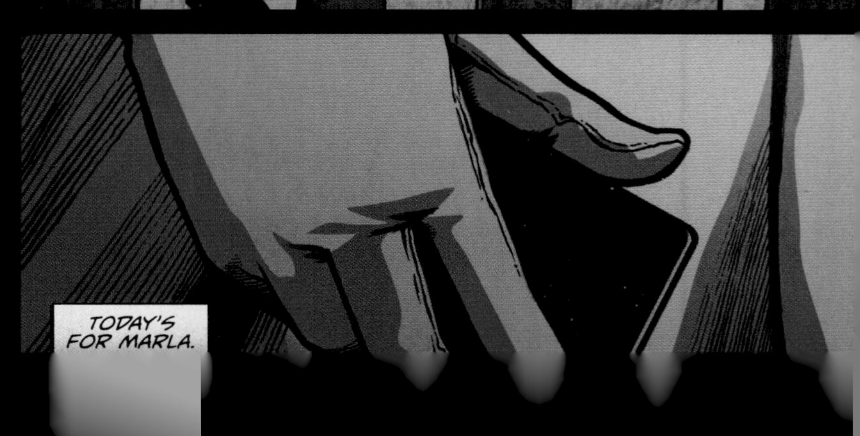
TODAY'S FOR MARLA.

KLIKK

DUNHILL CEMETERY

JUST A LITTLE FLICKER OF ONE OF THE MEMORIES I RECALLED LAST NIGHT.
A FUNERAL.
BUT I WASN'T CRASHING THAT ONE...I REMEMBER THE PAIN OF IT. UNBEARABLE.

THE MAN WITH HIS HANDS ON MY SHOULDERS...WAS THAT MY FATHER?

WAS THE FUNERAL FOR MY MOTHER?
WILLIAM JESUS VASQUEZ
LOVING SON AND BROTHER
REST IN PEACE
KLIKK
WILLIAM JESUS VASQUEZ

I DON'T REMEMBER.
AND PART OF ME IS GLAD. I DON'T WANT THE PAIN.

YOU'RE HER, AREN'T YOU?
TREY! I GOT HER!
THE BITCH IS OVER HERE!
INSIDE ME, I CAN FEEL MARLA'S FEAR AND BETRAYAL. THESE WERE HER BIG BROTHER'S CLOSEST FRIENDS.
AND SUDDENLY I'M DONE BEING AFRAID.

Shit.
SHE'S RUNNING FOR IT! TREY...
...GET YOUR ASS OVER HERE!
GRAY
NO POINT IN RUNNING, BITCH. NO EXIT BACK THIS WAY. YOU'RE DONE.

NOT EVEN CLOSE.
DAMN IT.
SHE'S GOING OVER THE BACK WALL ONTO...WHAT IS IT? CHESTNUT STREET? YOU GOT HER?
BA DOOP BA DOOP
WHAT THE HELL? MY PHONE KEEPS...
...I'VE GOT ALL THESE TEXTS...
BA DOOP BA DOOP

OMG, ANA...LOOK AT THIS.
NO WAY. YOU SICK FREAKS.
ANITA...
...I KNOW WHERE MARLA IS.

THERE! SHE'S RIGHT THERE!
I SEE HER!
BA DEEP BA DEEP
VRRRRMMM
WE GOTTA MOVE FAST. GET HER IN THE CAR.
BA DEEP BA DEEP
VRRRRMMMM

SSKKRRREEEE
GET IN THE CAR, GIRL.
WE'RE GONNA HAVE A TALK.
SHIT, MAN... I RECOGNIZE THIS CHICK.
CERISE, WE GOTTA GO!
WE GOTTA RUN!

huff huff
LISTEN!
LISTEN TO ME!
MARLA KEPT HER PHONE ON THAT NIGHT...FILMED THE WHOLE THING. I JUST GOT A TEXT WITH THE VIDEO, FROM MARLA'S PHONE!

SHE'S NOT THE ONLY ONE.
...CHESTNUT STREET, RIGHT BEHIND THE CEMETERY.
THEY'RE TRYING TO KILL A GIRL! HURRY!

YOU DID THIS! WHO ELSE DID YOU SEND IT--
PLEASE, CERISE. WE GOTTA GO!

WE'RE GOING, LINA. BUT SHE'S COMING WITH US.
NO, NO. PLEASE, LORD, PROTECT HER.
unhgfff
NO. NOT AGAIN.

KRAKK
ungghh
urkkh
WHAPP
CHRIST'S SAKE. I GOT TO DO EVERYTHING MYSELF.
WHO THE HELL *ARE* YOU?
WHY DON'T YOU *SAY* SOMETHING?
YOU'D BEST KEEP YOUR HANDS OFF THAT GIRL.
I'VE ALREADY CALLED THE POLICE!

SSKKRRREEE
Come on, now. Hurry!
I'M IN! GO!
NO, WAIT!
ESTEBAN, PLEASE!

POLICE
URRRRMMM

POLICE
JUST GO!
SHIT!
GO WHERE?
C 30
HIGHWAY PATROL

WHAT HAPPENED TO THE OTHER GIRL, MA'AM? THE ONE THEY WERE BEATING ON?

I SAW HER RUN OFF BEHIND THE NEIGHBOR'S HOUSE, OFFICER. PROBABLY A COUPLE OF STREETS AWAY BY NOW.
POOR THING, I THOUGHT THEY MIGHT KILL HER.
YOU GOT NO REASON TO HOLD US! WE DIDN'T DO NUTHIN'!
DETECTIVE, HAVE A LOOK AT THIS.
WHAT THE HELL'S GOING ON HERE?
WILLIAM JESUS VASQUEZ
LOVING SON AND BROTHER
REST IN PEACE

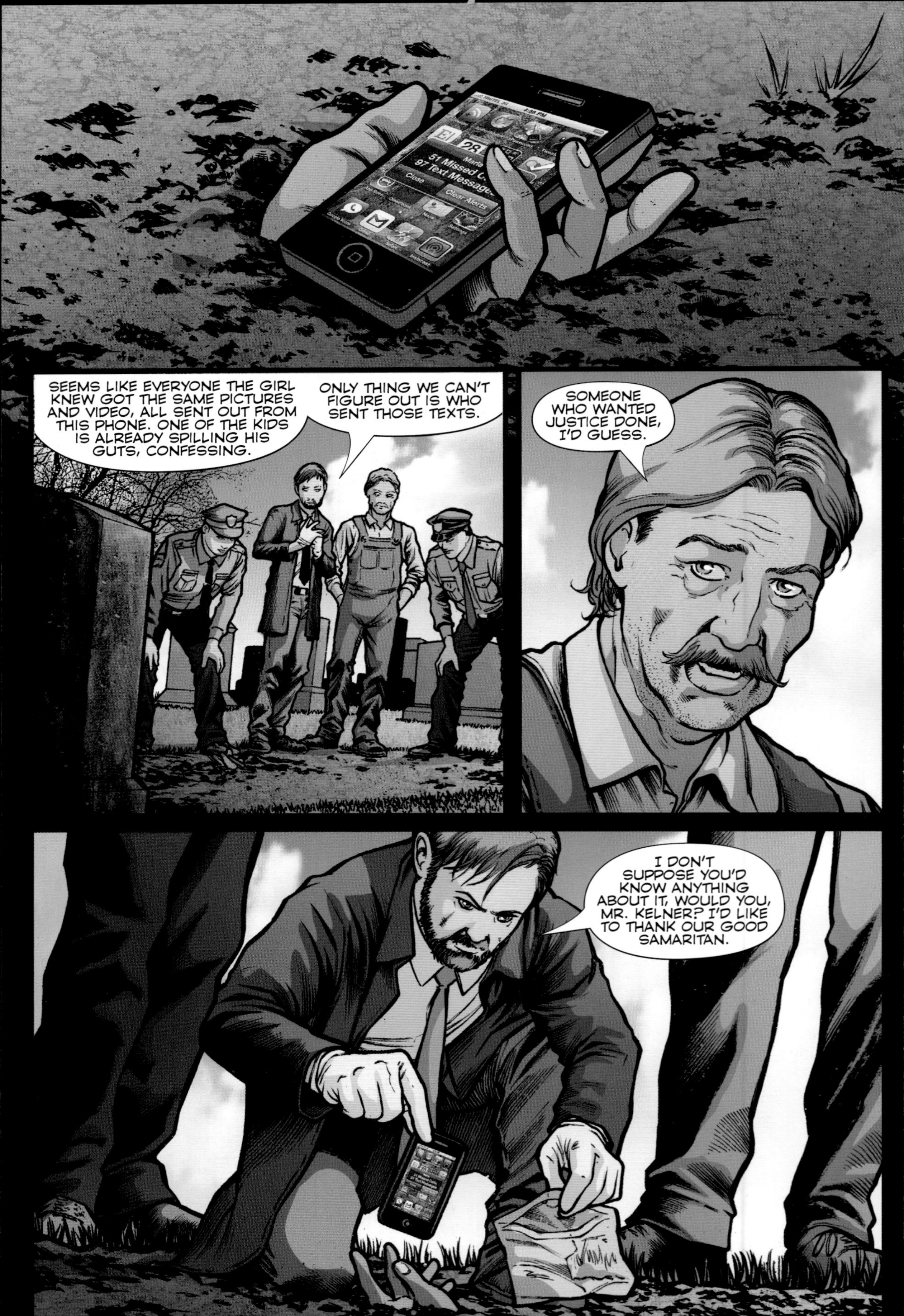
51 Missed Calls
97 Text Messages
Close
Clear Alerts
SEEMS LIKE EVERYONE THE GIRL KNEW GOT THE SAME PICTURES AND VIDEO, ALL SENT OUT FROM THIS PHONE. ONE OF THE KIDS IS ALREADY SPILLING HIS GUTS, CONFESSING.
ONLY THING WE CAN'T FIGURE OUT IS WHO SENT THOSE TEXTS.
SOMEONE WHO WANTED JUSTICE DONE, I'D GUESS.
I DON'T SUPPOSE YOU'D KNOW ANYTHING ABOUT IT, WOULD YOU, MR. KELNER? I'D LIKE TO THANK OUR GOOD SAMARITAN.

IT'S NOT YOU, IS IT?
YOU KIDDING ME, DETECTIVE?
I'M TOO OLD FOR SNEAKING AROUND.
I'VE HEARD STORIES ABOUT A GHOST IN DUNHILL CEMETERY.
YOU EVER SEE ANYTHING LIKE THAT?
CAN'T SAY I HAVE. NO, SIR...
...ALL THE GHOSTS IN DUNHILL CEMETERY ARE AT REST.
COUNTY POLICE

CALEXA?
I'm here, Lucinda...
AND I THINK IT'S TIME FOR US TO TALK.

I DIDN'T KNOW IF YOU'D EVER TELL ME HOW YOU ENDED UP IN THE CEMETERY.
I GUESS I WAS AFRAID THAT IF I TALKED ABOUT IT, YOU'D HAVE TO DO SOMETHING ABOUT IT.
IS THAT WHAT THIS IS? YOU'RE READY TO CHANGE THINGS?
I DON'T THINK SO. NOT YET. BUT I'M READY TO TRUST SOMEONE. THAT ISN'T EASY FOR ME.
GO ON, THEN, DEAR. TELL YOUR STORY.
I'LL DO ALL I CAN TO BE WORTHY OF YOUR TRUST.
THE FIRST THING I REMEMBER IS DYING...

MARLA'S MEMORIES ARE MOSTLY FADED NOW.
NOT GONE, EXACTLY, BUT THEY NO LONGER FEEL LIKE **MY** MEMORIES.
BUT IT ISN'T UNTIL THE FUNERAL THAT SHE...
OOH.
CAREFUL THERE, MISS.
...LEAVES ME.
THANK YOU SO MUCH.
DON'T MENTION IT. GRIEF GETS THE BETTER OF US ALL SOMETIMES.
ARE YOU ALL RIGHT, DEAR?
IT'S STRANGE...

...BUT I'M GOING TO MISS HAVING HER AROUND.

MARLA TERESA VASQUEZ
LOVING DAUGHTER AND SISTER
REST IN PEACE
WILLIAM JESUS VASQUEZ
LOVING SON AND BROTHER
REST IN PEACE

GOOD WORK, BOYS. SOON AS YOU FINISH WITH THE SOD, YOU CAN KNOCK OFF FOR TODAY. WHY NOT GET YOURSELVES A DRINK ON ME?
THAT'S NICE OF YA, TONY. I KNOW I COULD USE A DRINK OR TWO. THE YOUNG ONES ARE ALWAYS HARD.

RCL
YOU CAN COME OUT NOW, YOU KNOW.
I AIN'T GONNA BITE.
I SAW YOU AT THE FUNERAL THIS MORNING WITH THAT OLD LADY. I'M GLAD TO SEE YOU MADE A FRIEND.

NO? NOT COMIN' OUT?
OKAY, DARLIN'. ANOTHER DAY, THEN.

BUT IT MIGHT INTEREST YOU TO KNOW I PICKED UP AN EXTRA PACKAGE OF THOSE MINT CHOCOLATE COOKIES THAT KEEP VANISHING FROM MY KITCHEN.
I DO LIKE THOSE COOKIES.
OR WAS IT YOU WHO LIKED THEM, MARLA?
I GUESS I'LL FIGURE IT OUT. FIGURE ME OUT.
PAUL BLAKE R.I.P.
DREW MARSHALL REST IN PEACE
THE IMPORTANT THING IS THAT I'M STILL HERE. STILL ABOVE GROUND, DRAWING BREATH.
FOR TODAY, THAT'S ENOUGH.
MARLA TERESA VASQUEZ
LOVING DAUGHTER AND SISTER
REST IN PEACE
WILLIAM
LOVING
R

Read on for a script excerpt from
the next original graphic novel by
Charlaine Harris and Christopher Golden

Cemetery Girl

BOOK TWO: INHERITANCE

Coming soon from InkLit!

PAGE FOUR:

Panel one: Later. A shot of Lucinda's house from outside, a different angle than before and closer up. Starry sky above. The windows are all dark.

Panel two: In the bedroom she slept in at some point in book one, Calexa is asleep. The room has been made much more homey since then, with a plant and nicer bedding. She looks feverish, having kicked the covers partway off.

1/CALEXA/CAP: *I don't see Marla Vasquez in my dreams anymore. Truth is, I don't usually have dreams . . .*

Panel three: A dream/flashback. Let's do something with these panels to make clear they're not the real world. In this panel, Calexa is being injected with the serum we've hinted at, looking up in shock, realizing what has been done to her.

2/CALEXA/CAP: *For me, it's all nightmares.*

Panel four: Still in dream/flashback, she is punching someone who we see only in dream-silhouette—please try to make the person as difficult to pinpoint as possible, so it's not even clear if it's a male or female. They're in a lab, though we don't want to show what kind of lab.

3/CALEXA/CAP: *Mostly about the night I died.*

Panel five: Dream/flashback. Calexa being punched in the gut (let's see the fist but not its owner).

4/CALEXA/CAP: *If I could just see his face . . . But in my dream he's always in darkness . . .*

PAGE FIVE:

Panel one: Dream/flashback. Calexa being slapped hard.

1/CALEXA/CAP: *. . . always striking from the shadows.*

Panel two: Dream/flashback. Calexa crashing against a counter where there are racks of ampoules of some kind of drug. She's down on one knee, looking drugged out, turning back up toward her attacker (toward us, really).

2/CALEXA: *Why are . . . ? Why would you . . . ?*

Panel three: Dream/flashback. Calexa in a car trunk, looking dead, in the rain. (Another angle on something from book one.)

Panel four: Dream/flashback. Calexa tumbling down the slope in the rain (from book one).

3/CALEXA/CAP: *And then the dream always changes.*

Panel five: Dream/flashback. Calexa standing in the middle of the cemetery in the rain, looking around fearfully, hearing voices.

4/CALEXA/CAP: *It isn't about me anymore. It's about them.*

5/VOICE #1: *. . . Calexa . . . Help us, Calexa . . .*

PAGE SIX:

Panel one: Dream/flashback. SPLASH!!! Similar to last panel on previous page, but now Calexa is surrounded by the ghosts of the dead rising from their graves. They've all got their hands up, reaching toward her, pleading, and she looks terrified.

> **1/CALEXA/CAP:** *All the people like Marla, whose spirits have never really been laid to rest . . . whose ghosts are uneasy because the true stories of their deaths have yet to be told.*
>
> **2/VOICE #2:** *. . . Help us, Calexa . . .*
>
> **3/VOICE #3:** *. . . Like you helped Marla . . .*
>
> **4/VOICE #1:** *. . . Help us rest . . .*